my BIG DOG

by Janet Stevens and Susan Stevens Crummel
illustrated by Janet Stevens

 A GOLDEN BOOK • NEW YORK

Text © 1999 by Janet Stevens and Susan Stevens Crummel. Illustrations © 1999 by Janet Stevens. All rights reserved under International and Pan-American Copyright Conventions. Published in the United States by Golden Books, an imprint of Random House Children's Books, a division of Random House, Inc., New York, and simultaneously in Canada by Random House of Canada Limited, Toronto. Originally published in 1999 in slightly different form by Golden Books Publishing Company, Inc. Golden Books, A Golden Book, Big Little Golden Book, the G colophon, and the distinctive gold spine are registered trademarks of Random House, Inc.
First Random House Edition 2005
Library of Congress Control Number: 2004020369
ISBN: 0-375-83297-1 (trade)—ISNB: 0-375-93297-6 (lib. bdg.)
www.goldenbooks.com
PRINTED IN MALAYSIA
10 9 8 7 6 5

My name is Merl and I am a cat,
a very *special* cat.

Inside my house, my PUR-R-R-R-fect house, everything is MINE!

MY DISH

MY SOFA

MY CHAIR

MY MOUSE

MY BED

The people in my house are cat people.
They love to pet me. Which I let them do.
Sometimes, when I feel like it.

YAWN. I'm tired. I've been awake since
breakfast. It's time for a nap.
Ah-h-h-h, so quiet, so nice, so peaceful,
so PURR-R-R-R-fect.

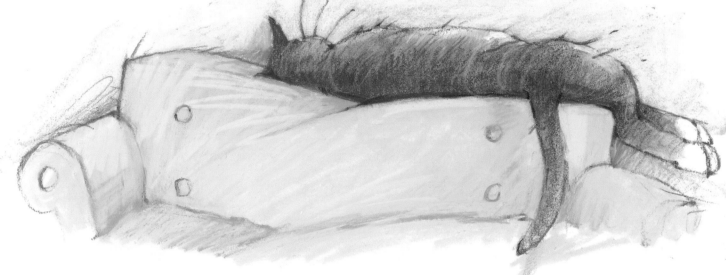

CRASH. THUD. WOOF. What's that?
What woke me up?
Shhh—I'm trying to sleep.
YIP. YIP. YIP.
Wait a minute.
I know those noises.

Those are puppy noises!
A puppy's in my house.
A wiggly, noisy,
slurpy, clumsy puppy!
That can't be.

Here come my people. They are
picking it up. They are talking to
it in cutesy-smootsey, lovey-dovey baby
voices. Uh-oh. It sees me.
Emergency alert—I have to hide!

I'll try hiding under the bed.

On top of the desk.

Inside a drawer.

That's one smart puppy. It found me.
PANT. PANT. SLURP.
It's licking me with its sloppy,
drooly tongue. YUCK.
I think it likes me. I think it wants to
be my friend. NO WAY. I am a cat and
it is a dog.

I have to get rid of it. I'll use my firm voice and tell it to leave. MEOW.

PANT. PANT. SLURP. There's that tongue again. This puppy won't listen. Bad puppy!

How about the doggie-out-the-door trick? Good puppy. Just follow these crumbs outside. Down the walk. Across the street. Uh-oh. I'm out of crumbs. And it's after me again with that big tongue.

Now what?

I've got it! I'll take it for a walk
and tie it to a tree.

Help! The puppy got away!
PANT. PANT. SLURP.
The big tongue is back.
Things can't get any worse!

Oh yes they can! Look at that puppy.
Each week, it gets bigger . . .

and **bigger** . . .

HELP! There's a huge dog in my house!

I guess I have no choice.
There's only one thing left to do—
LEAVE! I'll take
my mouse toy
and go.

Look. There's a nice lady.
I'll look real sad so she'll feel
sorry for me.
See? It worked. She's picking me up.
She's taking me home. She wants me.

SPLASH. WHIRRR. POOF.
She ruined me. I'm not a show cat. I don't like my fur fluffed and my claws painted. I'm Merl, a very special cat. NO WAY will I stay here. There must be a home for me somewhere. I'll keep looking.

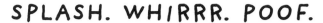

Hey, there's a sign,
CAT WANTED.
I'll look inside.

Nice house! No dogs, no bows—
I like this place. I'll go in and let
them know I'm here.

SLAM. SWAT. THUD.
What? No cats in the house?
I'm not a work cat! I can't
sleep in a barn and catch
mice. I'm Merl, a very
special cat. NO WAY will I
stay here. There must be a
home for me somewhere.
I'll keep looking.

Hey, look at those two kids playing. I'm sure they want a cat like me. I'll just rub against their legs and purr. PURR-R-R-R.
The boy is picking me up. "Nice kitty! I've always wanted a kitty!"

Help! The girl is grabbing me.
"My kitty!"
"No, mine!"
"Mine!"
"No, mine!"
Whoa. They both want me. STOP IT!
Put me down! I am NOT A TOY cat.
Don't play tug-of-war with me!
I'm Merl, a very special cat.

Where will I go?
Where will I live?
Look at me.
I'm a mess.
I can barely move.
I'm sore.
And I'm very tired.

I'll just climb into this empty box and rest a minute.

DRIZZLE. DRIZZLE.
Oh, dear. It's raining.
How I hate getting wet.
MEOW. MEOW. MEOW.

PANT. PANT. SLURP.
What's that?
Oh, no, not that big dog again!
It's picking me up.
Hey, put me down!

Where are you taking me?
This is no way for a cat to travel.
Let go of me!

Home! That big dog found
me and brought me home.
It misses me.
It needs me.
It likes me.
But I am a cat and
it is a dog.
A VERY BIG dog.

Could we be
friends? Is it
possible?
Hmmmm.
Maybe,
just MAYBE.

As long as it understands the rules. Inside my house, my PURR-R-R-fect house, everything is MINE!

MY DISH

MY SOFA

MY CHAIR

MY MOUSE

MY BED

and MY BIG DOG!